For Jo – N L
For Daniel – T W

LITTLE TIGER PRESS
An imprint of Magi Publications
1 The Coda Centre
189 Munster Road, London SW6 6AW
www.littletigerpress.com

First published in Great Britain 2010
This edition published 2011
Text copyright © Norbert Landa 2010
Illustrations copyright © Tim Warnes 2010

A CIP catalogue record for this book is
available from the British Library

Printed in China • LTP/1800/0268/0711

10 9 8 7 6 5 4 3 2 1

# The Great Monster Hunt

Norbert Landa    Tim Warnes

LITTLE TIGER PRESS
London

Early one morning, a funny noise woke up Duck. It sounded like, pshh pshh! and it came from right under her bed.

Duck was not quite sure what it was, and she was much too afraid to look.

Instead, she jumped out of bed
and ran for help.

"Pig!" Duck yelled. "There is something under my bed and it's making strange sounds. It goes, pshh pshh, **grrr**!"

"Pshh pshh, **grrr**?" asked Pig.
"Oh my! We need someone
really strong to help! Stay right
where you are!"

And Pig ran to find Bear.

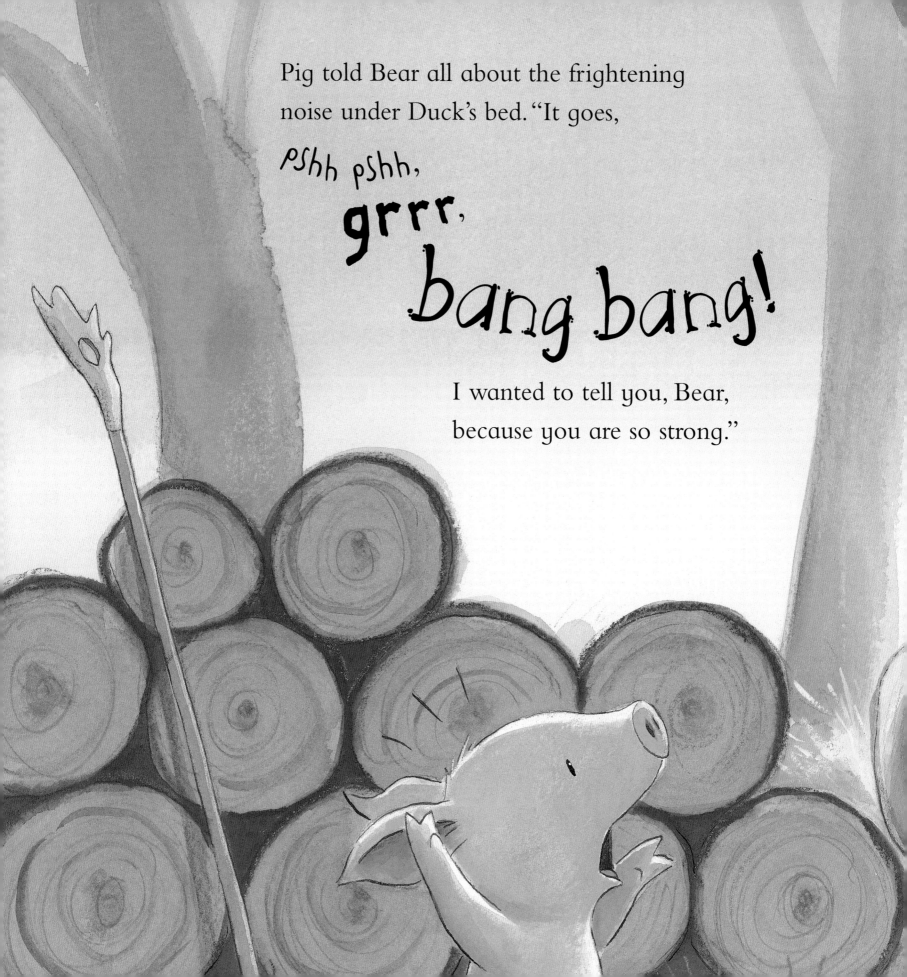

Pig told Bear all about the frightening noise under Duck's bed. "It goes,

pshh pshh,

grrr,

bang bang!

I wanted to tell you, Bear, because you are so strong."

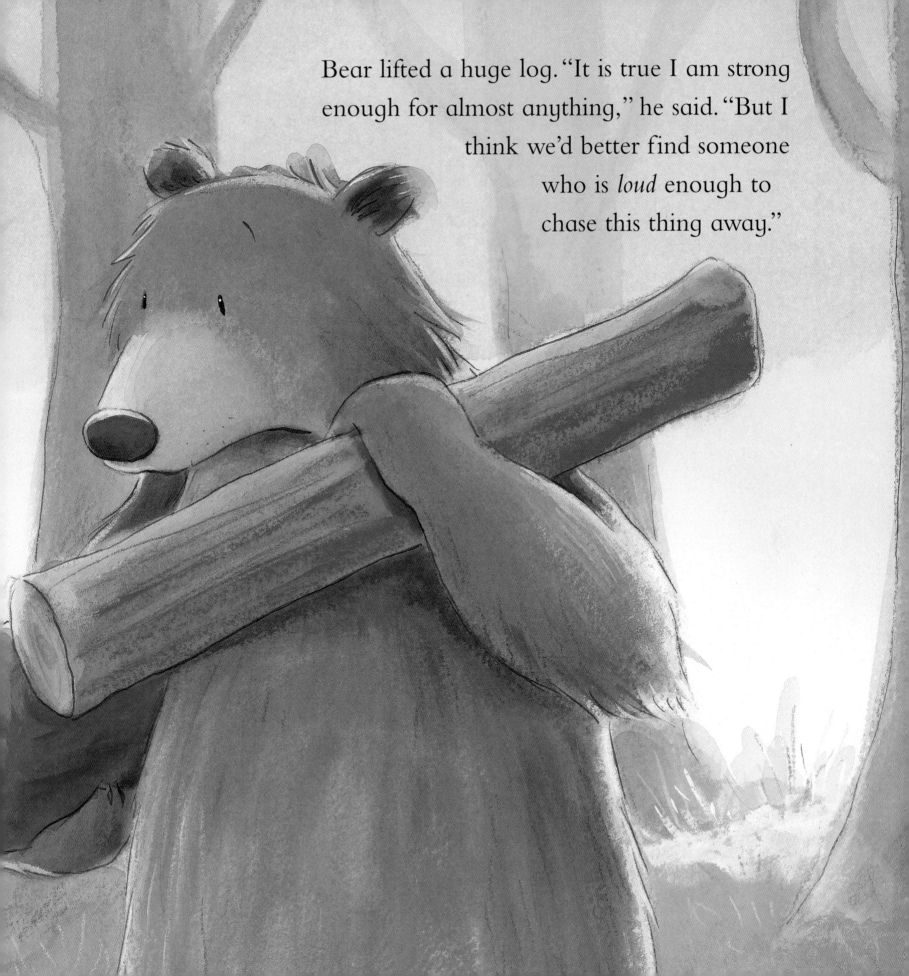

Bear lifted a huge log. "It is true I am strong enough for almost anything," he said. "But I think we'd better find someone who is *loud* enough to chase this thing away."

Bear told him the dreadful news about the terrifying thing under Duck's bed.

So they ran to find Wolf, who was about to start his early morning howling.

"It goes, pshh pshh, grrr, bang bang, pam pam —

all of the time!" Bear said.

"We thought you could help us frighten it away!"

"Oh yes, I can!" Wolf proudly said.

"There is no match for what
I can do. Just listen!

OWO ooooooo!

But maybe we also need help
from someone really clever."

So they ran to find Owl.

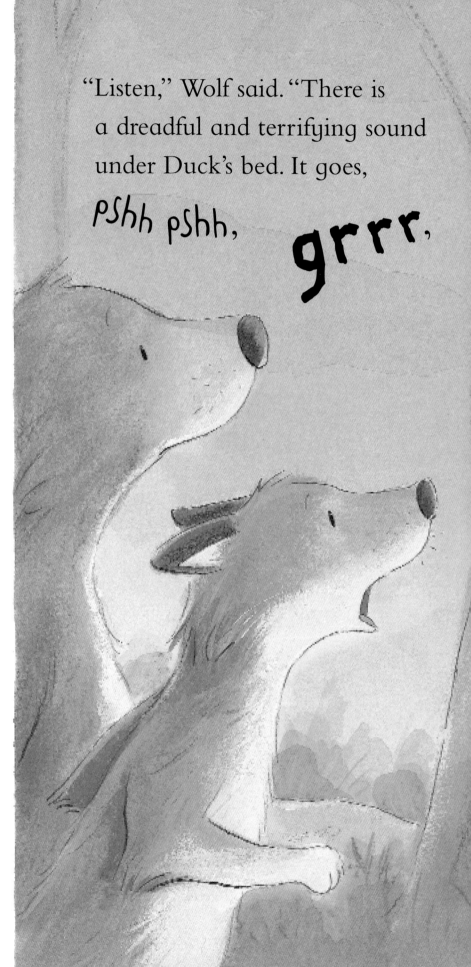

"Listen," Wolf said. "There is a dreadful and terrifying sound under Duck's bed. It goes,

pshh pshh,

grrr,

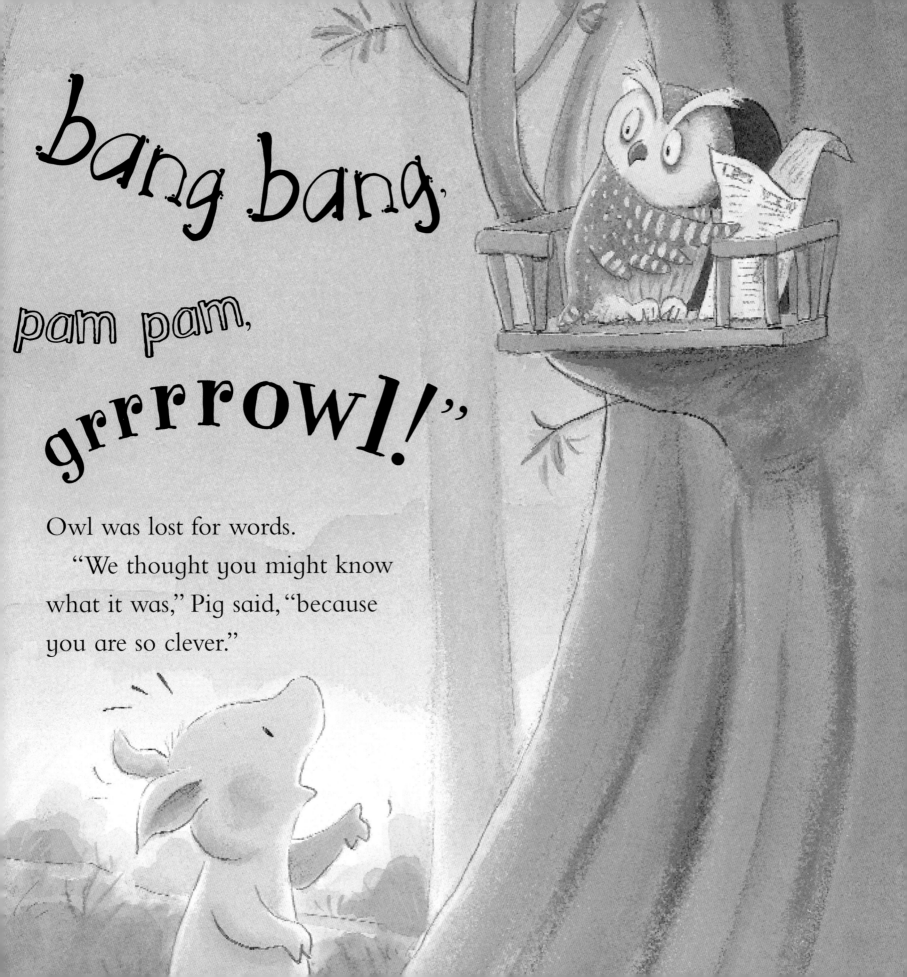

bang bang,

pam pam,

grrrrowl!"

Owl was lost for words.

"We thought you might know what it was," Pig said, "because you are so clever."

Owl said, "Clever, yes, that's what I am.
So I can tell you one thing:
# Duck is in great danger!"

Pig, Bear and Wolf huddled closer together.
"Are you sure?" they asked.

"Oh yes," Owl said. "Can you imagine anything
kind and cuddly making such a noise?"

"It must be a monster!" yelled Pig.
"Oh, what are we going to do?"

"The only way to deal with
a monster," Owl said, "is to trap it."

Clever Owl!

So the animals set about gathering rope and nets and useful pokey things. Then the four of them bravely set off towards Duck's house.

Owl led the way, because trapping the monster was his clever idea. Next came Wolf, howling loudly. Then came Bear, with his monster-buster stick. Last was Pig, clutching his great monster-catcher net.

Finally they arrived at Duck's house,
and flattened their ears against the door.
But no monstrous sound was heard – no
screaming nor crying nor calling for help.
    "Maybe we are too late?" whispered Bear.
    "Oh nooo!" Pig cried in despair.
    "Duck, are you there?" called Wolf.

Then the door slowly **creaked open** . . .

It was Duck. "You're here!" she said.

"Duck! You are in great danger!" whispered Bear.

"There's a monster under your bed!" cried Pig.

Duck looked fit to faint.

"A monster?" she whimpered.

"How do you know?"

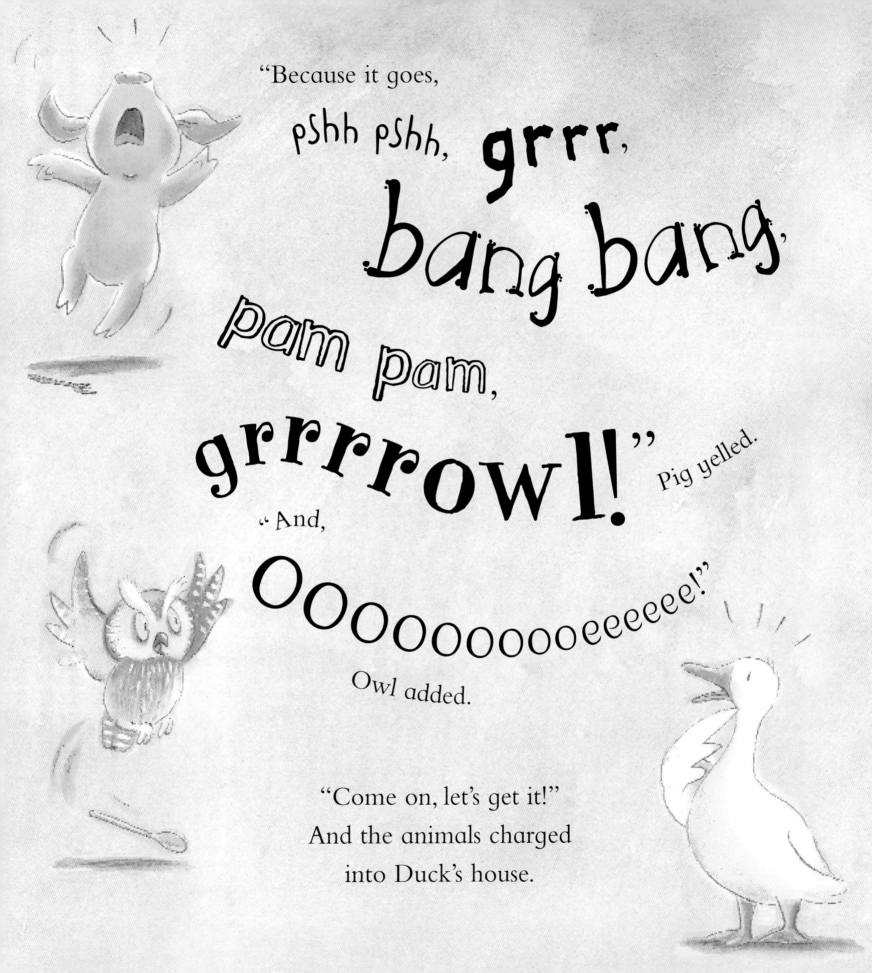

"Because it goes,

pshh pshh, **grrr**,

## bang bang,

pam pam,

# grrrrowl!" Pig yelled.

" And,

# OOOOOOOOOeeeee!"

Owl added.

"Come on, let's get it!"
And the animals charged
into Duck's house.

Up the stairs they crept, then they heard a sound.
PShh pShh! it went.
It came from right under Duck's bed.
Owl flashed his torch. The animals gasped.
They could not believe what they saw!

pshh pshh!

There, right under Duck's bed, was a tiny mouse,
snoring softly in its tiny bed, pShh pShh!
  "Well I never!" Duck whispered.
  "Do you know what we've just done?" Owl smiled.
  All feeling rather silly, the animals looked at
each other and giggled . . .

"We've just made a **monster** out of a mouse!"